Benji

SAVES CAMP

S0-EAQ-171

BENJI

Published by Scholastic Inc., *Publishers since 1920*. SCHOLASTIC and associated logos are trademarks and/or registered trademarks of Scholastic Inc.

The publisher does not have any control over and does not assume any responsibility for author or third-party websites or their content.

ISBN 978-1-338-26225-4

10 9 8 7 6 5 4 3 2 1   19 20 21 22 23

Printed in the U.S.A.   40
First printing 2019

Benji

SAVES CAMP

by Mary Tillworth

Scholastic Inc.

CHAPTER 1

Benji's stomach was growling. He could hear the rumbles through his matted golden fur as he trotted down the road. It had been two days since his last meal, when he had passed through a town with plenty of garbage cans to dig through. Now forests of maple and oak surrounded him, their leaves shimmering in the hot, humid afternoon air.

As his nails clicked against the black asphalt, Benji's head drooped. He had been on the road for a year, a wiry-haired mutt with a nose for adventure. He was used to uncertainty and hunger. The longest he had gone without food was four days, and he knew he still had time to find a stray donut or a patch of wild strawberries. But his nose was bone-dry. His tongue lay panting between his teeth. He had to find water. Soon.

As he rounded a bend in the road, he caught a glint of silver between the trees. His black-tipped ears perked up, and he swung off the hot pavement and into the woods. Picking his way through the ferns and bramble bushes, he moved closer to the gleaming reflection until he was standing on the shore of a wide lake.

Benji perched himself on the edge of a large rock jutting into the water. He bent his head down and drank. It tasted like pure heaven to him. After he had lapped up as much of the cold, clear liquid that he could, he leapt off the rock and plunged belly-first into the lake. His mouth broke open in a huge grin as his legs moved instinctively, keeping him afloat as he cooled down. He loved the feel of the water running through his fur. Even though it was only his first time swimming, he was already good at it.

As he paddled around, the smell of bacon suddenly flooded through his nostrils. Turning his head, Benji saw a cluster of wooden buildings perched at the far end of the lake. He knew what that meant. Food! He headed back to land and gave himself a vigorous shake. He took one final gulp of water and then headed toward the promise of lunch.

When he finally reached the wooden buildings, he went into sneak mode. Benji loved humans, but he knew that they were often not very happy with him when he upturned their garbage cans and ate their leftovers. He dropped to the ground and slunk carefully behind bushes and trees as he traced the scent of bacon to a large building. Benji looked around. When he didn't see any humans, he hurried over to the side of the building and jumped up to peer in one of the windows.

He saw tables and benches lined up in neat rows, with enough room for fifty people to eat. The tables had been set with plates and silverware. Benji realized that he was peering into some sort of dining hall. As he watched, an older teenager with cropped blond hair and stern blue eyes entered through a swinging door, holding a large bin full of rattling plastic cups. He set the bin down on one of the benches and began placing a cup next to each plate.

Benji dropped to all fours. As he headed toward the back of the building, the smell of bacon grew stronger. He spotted a screen door and went up to it. Lifting a paw, he quietly pulled the door open and slipped inside. His tail caught the door as it swung back, and it closed softly.

Benji found himself in a large kitchen with stainless-steel counters and a long island positioned in the center. Countless utensils hung down from hooks along the wall. There was a man standing with his back toward Benji, cheerily whistling to himself as he tossed pizza dough high in the air. Next to him, Benji saw two sheet pans on the counter.

Parchment paper dangled over the pans, glistening with grease. The smell of bacon was overwhelming.

A small, hungry whine escaped from Benji's throat. He could feel a full-on roar gathering in his stomach. But he couldn't get to the bacon without being seen. Just as he was figuring out how to distract the cook, the door from the dining hall swung open.

Benji ducked behind the island just as the teenager who had been setting tables came into the kitchen holding an empty bin.

"All the cups in place, Bobby?" the cook asked.

"Yeah." Bobby held up the bin. "Where do I put this?"

The cook set down the dough on a pizza pan and wiped his hands on his apron. "Follow me and I'll show you," he said. He took the bin from Bobby, and the two of them walked over to the far end of the kitchen.

Benji saw his chance. He ran over to the sheet pans and stood up on his hind legs. Using his front paws, he pulled one of the sheet pans over the edge of the counter until it tipped over completely, crashing to the floor with a bang. Slices of bacon rained down. Benji snatched as many pieces as he could and hightailed it out of the kitchen.

He had done it! He had found lunch! Running one way and then the other, Benji dodged and wove through the woods. Behind him, he could hear the cries of the cook and Bobby. As he ran, they grew fainter and fainter. When he finally dared to look back, he saw that the cook had given up and was returning to the kitchen. But Bobby was still on his tail, his eyes set with anger and determination.

Benji searched for a place to hide. Ahead of him, he saw a line of cabins. All the doors and windows appeared tightly closed, except for the last cabin, which had a door that was hanging slightly open. He bolted toward it, ran up the front steps, and nudged his way inside.

CHAPTER 2

It was quiet and cool in the cabin. As Benji began to munch on his hard-won lunch, he looked around. There were two sets of bunk beds lined against one wall, and a single bed pushed up against the corner of the opposite wall. Neat piles of clothes were stacked on the single bed, along with a worn blue book that looked as though it had been read many times over.

Benji heard a sound outside. He went to a window next to the cabin door and stood up on his hind legs to look through it. He saw a boy wearing a backward baseball cap with silky black hair sticking out from underneath it coming up the cabin steps. He was chewing a wad of gum and dragging a duffel bag almost as large as himself.

Benji wasn't sure how the kid would react to an

intruder in the cabin. He decided to play it safe and scrambled under one of the bunk beds to hide. He had just gotten out of sight when the door was pulled wide open. The boy entered and pulled his bag up to the bunk bed where Benji lay crouched. He plopped down on the bottom bunk, unzipped the bag, and began tossing piles of shirts and shorts onto the mattress.

A minute later, a boy with dark curly hair and playful eyes arrived, carrying a backpack that was about half the size of the first kid's duffel bag. He went to the remaining bottom bunk and hefted his backpack onto it to claim it. When he was done, he turned to the first kid. "*¿Qué tal?*" he said, and stuck out his hand. "Name's Manny."

"I'm Eddie." Eddie smacked his gum loudly. He didn't take Manny's hand. "Am I supposed to know who 'Kate Owl' is?"

Manny laughed. "No, *amigo*, '*Qué tal*' is Spanish for 'How's it going?'"

Eddie folded his arms. "I don't know Spanish, so speak English."

Manny shrugged and withdrew his hand. "And I don't know Chinese, but I'm open to trying."

Eddie glared at Manny. "People from China are Chinese. The language I speak is Mandarin."

Manny leaned forward. "You know, another phrase you could use is, *'¡A ver, relájate!'* That means 'Lighten up, will you?'"

Eddie's face turned red. Before he could respond, a quiet cough made the two boys turn their heads. There was a third camper in the room. He had come in so silently, neither boy had heard him.

"Hi," said the third camper. "I'm Tony." He stood by the doorway, a small backpack resting against his skinny legs. "Would either of you mind taking a top bunk? I'm afraid of heights."

"No way!" declared Eddie. He reached into his duffel bag and threw another heap of clothes on the bottom bunk. "I got here first, which means I get to pick."

"Sorry, Tony, but Eddie's right. First come, first served." Manny pointed to the bunk above his. "But you can have my top bunk if you want. I just saw a big spider crawling around on the top of the other bunk."

Eddie jumped. "Ugh! I hate spiders! Where is it?"

Manny's eyes grew wide. "Hold very still, Eddie. It's . . . right . . . next to you."

Eddie stood stock-still and squeezed his eyes closed. "Make it go away! Make it go away!" he pleaded.

Manny reached into his pocket and pulled out a gigantic plastic spider. He carefully put it on Eddie's shoulder. "It's on you!" he screamed.

Eddie let out a bloodcurdling cry and batted frantically at himself. The spider fell onto the floor, and Manny went to work stomping on it. "Don't worry, Eddie, I got you," he called.

As Manny lifted his foot, Eddie looked down. "It's fake!" he cried. "You dingbat!"

"What's going on? Why are you guys being so loud?" yelled a new voice. "It's only the first day of camp, and you're gonna get us all in trouble!"

The three boys turned to see a fourth camper entering the cabin. He was staring at them with worried green eyes underneath a mop of red hair that seemed to glow in the late afternoon sun. "I'm Jake. I'm in Bunkhouse Ten with the rest of you, and I just saw our camp counselor a minute ago. He's coming soon and he's gonna be real mad if we're all fighting when he gets here!" He sniffed the air. "And by the way, who's eating bacon? I was told that dinner was after orientation."

Manny picked up the spider and shoved it in his pocket. "Wasn't me."

Eddie crossed his arms. "Not me."

"Not me, either." Tony took a sniff and followed the scent to the bottom of one of the bunk beds. He pointed. "Look." The tip of a golden-haired tail was sticking out from under Eddie's bunk.

All four boys dropped to the ground and peered underneath the bunk. Benji stared back at them. Most of the bacon he had snatched from the kitchen was gone, but there were still bits stuck to the hair on his chin. He knew this was the moment when he had to win the boys over. He gave them the biggest, goofiest smile he could muster and thumped his tail. His tongue stuck out and he licked Eddie's knee.

"There's a dog under my bed!" cried Eddie.

"Wow! We've got a dog!" Manny cheered.

"Whose dog is this? Are dogs even allowed at camp?" asked Jake.

"I don't think this dog belongs to any of us," replied Tony. "He doesn't have a collar. And I'm almost sure that dogs aren't allowed."

"Well, then, we've got to keep him hidden," said Manny. He reached under the bunk and gently petted Benji's head. "He can be our mascot."

"You know, I've always wanted a dog," Eddie admitted. He scratched Benji's hind leg as Benji thumped his tail even harder.

"Me too," said Tony. He looked at Jake. "You okay with keeping this dog a secret?"

"Oh boy, oh boy, you know we could get into so much trouble if he's found out." Jake looked at the other three boys. He sighed heavily. "Fine, I won't rat on you guys. But if this dog does one wrong thing, he's out of here!"

"Deal." Manny held out his hand. "C'mon. We've got to take an oath."

One by one, the other boys piled their hands on top of Manny's.

"Now repeat after me," said Manny. "We solemnly swear to keep this dog hidden and safe."

"We solemnly swear to keep this dog hidden and safe," chanted the boys.

"And if we don't, may our arms fall out of their sockets and our brains ooze out of our skulls," continued Manny.

"That's so gross!" said Jake.

"If you really mean to take care of this dog, then you've got to say it," said Manny.

"Okay, okay," grumbled Jake.

"And if we don't, may our arms fall out of their sockets and our brains ooze out of our skulls," the boys repeated. They pressed their hands down, then flung them up high to seal the promise.

Jake glanced out the window. "Guys, the camp counselor is coming up the steps!"

Eddie dug into his duffel bag and hurriedly pulled out a handful of underwear. He heaved them onto Benji's tail, then bent down and patted Benji. "No wagging," he warned.

Benji thumped his tail one last time, and then he lay still just as the door opened and the older teenager from the kitchen marched inside.

CHAPTER 3

The teenager closed the cabin door, blocking off any chance Benji could have had to escape. He stood in front of the campers, his arms folded tightly across his chest. "Welcome to Camp Lakewood. My name is Bobby, and I'll be your counselor for the week. Now, what are all of your names?"

After Eddie, Manny, Tony, and Jake had introduced themselves, Bobby raised his eyebrows at the messy piles of clothes Eddie had strewn everywhere. "If you're thinking that camp is like home and you can just put your stuff any place you please, think again. You will be living with three other boys and myself, and you will need to pick up after yourself." He nodded toward the pile of underwear that was covering Benji's tail. "Whose are those?"

Eddie jumped in front of the pile. "Mine."

"Pick them up," said Bobby.

"But . . . but . . ." Eddie stuttered.

"Now," Bobby ordered. He glared at Eddie.

As Eddie slowly crouched down and began to pick up a pair of underwear, Manny jumped in front of Bobby. "Hey! Is that a spider I see?" he said, pointing behind Bobby.

"Where?" Bobby turned his head.

Manny gave Eddie a wink. As he ran to the far end of the cabin, Eddie grabbed all of his underwear and pushed Benji's tail completely under the bunk.

"Here it is!" Manny pretended to grab his plastic spider from the windowsill. He dangled it by one leg. "I've got it!" he called as he rushed to the door and flung the spider outside.

Bobby frowned. "Thanks for taking care of that." He turned back to the boys. "And thanks for picking up your underwear," he told Eddie. "You can put them in one of the two storage trunks that you'll find under your bed. The other will be for your bunkmate. Here, let me show you."

"I got it!" yelped Eddie. He dropped to the floor and hastily pulled out both of the trunks before Bobby could kneel down and look under the bunk bed. He pushed one toward Jake. "This one's for you," he said.

Manny and Tony pulled out their own trunks. As each of the boys put away their clothes, Bobby picked up the worn blue book on his bed and thumbed through it. When they were done, he held up the book and pointed to it. "This is the camp rule book. You will find a copy of it under your pillows. I expect you to read it completely by the end of the night, and throughout the week, you must always keep it on you. I will go over the basics with you."

Bobby began to pace the room like a drill sergeant. "Morning wake-up call is at six forty-five. Beds must be made and campers must be dressed and ready to go by seven fifteen. Breakfast is at seven thirty; camp activities start at eight on the dot. I expect each of you to be punctual. Lunch is at noon; dinner is at six. By eight, you will all be back at the bunkhouse. Floors must be swept and belongings tidied. Lights out at nine. Any questions?"

Manny raised his hands. "When do we actually get to have fun? It sounds like we're at boot camp, not sleepaway camp."

"You will have fun, but it will be scheduled," replied Bobby. "And most importantly, throughout the week you will be earning points toward the Camp Lakewood competition."

Eddie furrowed his eyebrows. "What's that?" he asked.

"Every time a bunkhouse arrives on time for an activity or wins a game, it will gain a certain number of points," replied Bobby. "At the end of the week, the bunkhouse that has the most points wins the Camp

Lakewood trophy, along with medals etched with each of our names." Bobby pointed to one of his bedposts. A pile of medals hung from it. "For the past four years, Bunkhouse Ten has always won, and I intend to win a fifth by the end of the week. It'll be the most wins for one bunkhouse in the history of the camp!"

"Wait. We're competing against other campers?" Jake shuddered. "But what if they sabotage us? What if things go horribly wrong and there's a blood feud? What if our children and our children's children wind up locked in endless battle against one another?"

"It'll be worth it. Life is about WINNING," Bobby declared. He raised his head and sniffed suddenly. "Do I smell bacon?"

The boys gave one another panicked looks.

"Uhh . . . no?" said Manny.

"There was a mutt who broke into the kitchen and made off with some bacon that was supposed to go on tonight's pizza dinner. I tried to chase it down, but I lost it somewhere near the cabin." Bobby narrowed his eyes. "It wouldn't be . . . *in* the cabin, now, would it?"

"Nope, we haven't seen a thing. No mutt, no bacon, nope, nope, nope," sputtered Jake.

"Well, the only place it could hide if it were in here is under one of the bunks," said Bobby. He walked over to Eddie and Jake's bunk and began to crouch down.

"I'll check!" cried Eddie. He dropped to the floor. His eyes met Benji's for a moment. Then he quickly pushed his way back up to standing. "No dog at all!"

Bobby raised his eyebrows. "Are you sure?"

"Super sure," promised Eddie.

In the distance, a bell gonged.

"That's the dinner bell. We have to be at the dining hall in ten minutes," said Bobby.

"I'll bet the bacon smell is coming from there," said Tony.

Bobby nodded. "I guess you're right. Let's go, Bunkhouse Ten," he called.

The boys hurried to the dining hall and quietly ate their dinner. When Bobby got up to help with the dishes, the boys huddled together.

"We've got to come up with a plan to get the dog out of there. Bobby could discover him at any second," said Jake.

"Plus, he probably has to pee," added Manny.

Tony spoke up. "I've got an idea. We head back to the bunkhouse before Bobby and get the dog outside. We'll make him a little bed with some of our clothes near the cabin. Early tomorrow, we'll sneak out. If he's still hanging around, we'll build him a little doghouse off in the woods. We can get some tools and wood scraps from the woodworking shop."

Eddie smiled. "Sounds like a plan."

CHAPTER 4

"Welcome to *la casa del perro*," Manny whispered loudly. "It's your new doghouse, boy!"

In the early morning light, Benji cocked his ears and stared at the misshapen mass of wooden boards held together by hundreds of crazily hammered-in nails. It was leaning badly to one side. He gave a woof and trotted in happily. He didn't care that the shelter looked like it was about to fall down on him. The boys had built it with love, and he was going to let them know that he appreciated it.

Tony was kneeling next to the entrance of the doghouse holding a hammer. He reached over and gave Benji a pat on the head. He scooped up the left-over nails and shoved them in his pocket. Then he stood up, dusted off his hands, and slipped the hammer in a loop in his jeans. "It's not perfect, but it'll hold," he announced, looking at the doghouse.

Jake checked his watch. "It's almost six thirty," he said. "We've got to get back to the bunkhouse before Bobby wakes up."

"Just a sec." Eddie smacked a new stick of gum as he opened a small backpack and took out a thick slice of pizza he had saved from dinner the night before. "Breakfast time, buddy," he told Benji.

Benji gave a happy bark. He opened his mouth and wolfed the slice down. He licked his chops. Then he licked Eddie's hand.

Eddie laughed. "That tickles." He scratched behind Benji's ears with his other hand. "You know, we should give you a name."

Jake tapped his watch. "We should get going; that's what we should do."

"All right." Eddie zipped up his backpack and hefted it onto his shoulders.

As the boys started back toward the bunkhouse, Benji leapt out of his shelter to follow them.

"No, no, no!" whispered Jake. "You gotta stay!"

Benji drew his ears back. A small whine escaped from his throat. He didn't want the boys to leave.

"Stay, boy," said Tony, softly but firmly.

Benji reluctantly padded back to his shelter. He could tell by Tony's tone of voice that the boys needed him to keep put. Once the boys had left, he settled down among the leaves and sighed. His eyes blinked more and more slowly. They had almost completely closed when he spotted something lying in the dirt.

It was a copy of the camp rule book. Benji realized it must have fallen out of Eddie's backpack when he had opened it to give Benji the pizza slice.

Benji remembered that the evening before, when he had been stuck under the bunk bed, he had watched Bobby hold up his copy of the rule book and point to it several times. He had a feeling that Eddie would get into trouble if Bobby discovered the book was missing.

Benji couldn't let that happen. He got to his feet and picked up the rule book with his front teeth, trying carefully not to get it wet. He found his way easily back to Bunkhouse Ten, using his nose to detect the scent of Eddie's chewing gum.

Once he arrived, Benji trotted up the steps and jumped up to look in the window. He almost dropped the book in surprise. His nose was an inch from the back of Bobby's T-shirt. The camp counselor had opened the windows and was standing next to them, inspecting the boys' bunks.

"Beds made, check. Clothes put away, check." Bobby looked at his watch. "Six forty-five, check. Let's go to breakfast. Everybody have their rule book?"

Tony, Manny, and Jake held up their rule books. Eddie looked around. "It must be in my backpack," he muttered. He unzipped his pack and rummaged inside. His face grew pale. "I put it here last night; I'm sure of it."

Benji nudged the rule book onto the windowsill and poked his head around Bobby's waist so the campers could see him.

Tony spotted him first. His eyes grew wide.

Bobby frowned. "Is there a ghost at the window?" he asked. He turned around.

Nothing was there except the little blue rule book resting on the windowsill.

Underneath the camp steps, Benji breathed a sigh of relief. He had ducked down and scampered out of sight just in time. He did not want a second encounter with the boys' camp counselor.

Bobby picked up the rule book and handed it to Eddie. "You must have left it here last night. Don't lose it again," he warned.

Eddie nodded quickly and grabbed the rule book.

As the boys headed to breakfast, Benji watched them from his hiding spot. He was glad that he had been able to keep Eddie from getting into hot water. His eyelids began to droop. A minute later, he was curled up, his tail tucked between his legs, fast asleep.

Benji woke to the sound of feet shuffling up the steps. He blinked the sleep out of his eyes and decided to risk peeking his head out. He saw Eddie, Manny,

Tony, and Jake on the porch about to go into the cabin—but no Bobby. He gave a happy yelp and ran to meet his friends.

Eddie scooped him up in a giant bear hug. "Thanks for saving my butt this morning," he told Benji. "Now, let's get you inside before anyone else sees you." He carried Benji into the bunkhouse and set him down on the wooden floor. "We've got break time for an hour before Bobby comes and gets us for a volleyball game."

"Did anyone save the pooch some lunch?" Tony asked. "I've got half a peanut butter and jelly sandwich, but that's it."

Manny pulled a chocolate bar from his backpack. "I didn't save any lunch, but he can have this."

"No!" cried Jake. "Dogs aren't supposed to have chocolate. It makes them sick and throw up and go into seizures and stuff."

"Huh. I never knew that." Manny looked through his backpack again. He held up a bag of potato chips. "These okay?"

Jake nodded. "Yeah, I think so."

Manny opened the bag and dropped the chips to the floor. Benji crunched down on them, and then snuffled around to lick up the crumbs. When he was done, Tony fed him the peanut butter sandwich. It barely lasted one second.

"I like having a dog," Eddie said. "It's nice to feel

like he's kind of taking care of us, and we're taking care of him. Like, he returned my rule book, and we keep him fed."

"We still need to name him," said Tony.

"Maybe he already has a name," Manny suggested. He crouched down in front of Benji. "Are you a . . . Rover? Spot? Max? Buddy? Rocky? Duke?"

"He doesn't have a name. He's a stray," said Eddie.

"Tucker?" continued Manny, ignoring Eddie. "Charlie? Jack? Ben?"

Benji gave a half woof, half growl.

"Ben?" Manny raised his eyebrows.

Benji half woofed again, and then whined.

"Maybe you're half right," said Tony. He looked at Benji. "Are you a Benjamin? Benny? Benji?"

Benji grinned and gave a full-on bark.

"I think his name is Benji!" declared Tony.

"Well, Benji, how would you like to help us play a prank on Bobby?" Manny asked. He bent under his bunk bed and pulled out his storage trunk. He opened it and took out a tape recorder. "I just need you to bark for me a couple of times."

"How are you going to do that?" asked Jake.

"Watch and learn." Many tipped his head back and howled like a werewolf. *"Aaaoooo! Aaaoooo!"* He clicked on the tape recorder.

Benji barked loudly. Then he threw his head back and howled, too.

Manny clicked off the tape recorder. "Got it!" He turned to the other boys. "Tonight, after lights out, I'm going to play this. Bobby'll think that there's a ghost dog in the cabin!"

"Speaking of Bobby, I see him coming," said Jake. "We've got to get Benji out of here!"

"Quick!" Tony opened the back cabin window. "He can go out this way."

Eddie lifted Benji up and hauled him to the window. "Go on, little guy," he instructed.

Benji leapt through the open window and landed softly at the back of the cabin. He was happy to be part of the boys' world, even if he had to keep hidden. With his belly full of chips and peanut butter, he spent the afternoon swimming along the calm, clear lake as he watched the boys playing volleyball on the beach in the distance.

After his long swim, he returned to his little shelter and curled up for the night. He slept soundly, never hearing the yell of surprise that filled Bunkhouse Ten an hour after lights out, or the muffled giggles of the boys who had pulled off a joke well played.

CHAPTER 5

Benji woke to a gray and cloudy morning well rested and content. When he was finally ready to get up, he stretched his legs out in front of him and yawned lazily. He was about to head to Bunkhouse Ten when he saw the boys in the distance. They were coming toward him and carrying large backpacks. Benji was about to woof a greeting and join them when he saw a tall figure with a stern, familiar face. Bobby was heading up the rear.

Benji scrambled out of the doghouse and made a beeline for the nearest big oak. He stood, hidden, until Bobby and the boys had passed him. Then, as quietly as he could, he followed them.

As he went through the woods, Benji thought about how he could have visited another bunkhouse that morning. He could have tried to make friends with other campers in hopes of finding breakfast. But Benji didn't want to be friends with any old campers—he wanted to be friends with Eddie, Manny, Tony, and Jake. They were *his* campers. And as long as he kept out of sight of Bobby, he knew he could eventually come out and play with them. He figured that wherever they were going, it wouldn't be far.

But he was wrong. It felt like hours before Bobby called for everyone to halt. When he did, all the campers dropped their packs like sacks of cement and stood gasping for air.

"How long until we reach the campsite?" Jake asked Bobby.

"About another mile," answered Bobby. "We've only gone three so far."

"It feels like three thousand," groaned Manny. "I've never carried this much weight. My shoulders are killing me."

Eddie found a water bottle in his pack and unscrewed the cap. He took a big gulp. "Are you sure that people do this for fun?" he panted.

"Camping out is great," Bobby replied huffily. "I know you're all from the city and you've never done it before, but trust me, it's really useful. You'll learn a lot about survival. How to build a fire, how to make a shelter, how to cook dinner, and how to survive the night in the woods. Plus, you'll learn how to work together. You never know when these skills might come in handy. And for every camping task you complete, we get points."

"I don't care about points, and unless there's a zombie apocalypse, we don't need to learn all this," groaned Manny.

"Well, I *do* care about points. And if there *is* a zombie apocalypse someday, maybe you'll thank me for teaching you the skills to survive it," snapped Bobby. He adjusted the pack on his back. "Break's over. Let's get going."

The boys struggled into their backpacks and kept going. Benji trailed quietly behind them, keeping low in the surrounding bushes, until the forest gave way and they finally arrived at an open meadow.

"This is the campsite," announced Bobby. "First thing I'm going to teach you is how to set up your shelters." He looked up at the sky. "Judging from the clouds, we're going to need them soon." He opened his pack and pulled out a tarp, pieces of nylon string, and a handful of stakes. After finding a two-foot stick, Bobby showed the boys how to build a makeshift tent by staking down the tarp and propping up one side with the stick. It took him ten minutes.

An hour later, it was raining steadily and Eddie's and Jake's tarps were still lying in sad piles on the ground. The two boys were still trying frantically to figure out how to tie knots in the nylon strings to stake down their tents. Manny's tarp was up, but the stick he had used to prop it up kept falling down. Only Tony's tarp tent was completely intact.

"We need to get on to the next task: building a fire," shouted Bobby through the rain.

"How are we going to light a fire when everything is soaked?" Manny asked.

Bobby nodded toward the woods. "Not everything is wet. Find a place that's covered by the tree foliage and look for some dead branches. Live branches are no good—they won't burn." He handed Manny a garbage bag. "Put the dead branches in here to keep them dry and bring them back to the camp. Get a partner to help you."

Manny pointed to Eddie. "I choose him."

"Fine." Bobby turned to Jake and Tony. "In the meantime, you two will make dinner."

As Bobby began to unpack camping stoves and pasta packages, Manny and Eddie tromped into the woods until they were out of sight of Bobby and the other boys.

Manny spotted a branch on the ground and picked it up. He wrinkled his nose and threw it down. "This is soaking wet." He sighed. "This stinks. I wish Benji was here."

When he heard his name, Benji gave a joyful bark and ran out from the bushes.

"Benji!" cried Manny. He dropped the garbage bag and wrapped Benji up in a big hug. "I missed you."

As soon as Manny set him down, Benji jumped up and woofed happily. He turned and leapt onto Eddie, knocking him over and covering his face in doggie kisses. He was so happy to see his campers again!

Eddie laughed and scratched the scruff around Benji's neck. "All right, all right. Good boy," he said. He stood up and picked up the garbage bag. "C'mon. Let's go find some firewood."

Benji trotted at the heels of Eddie and Manny. When Manny found a dead tree and began snapping off branches, Benji picked up stray pieces that had already broken off around the tree and brought them to Eddie, who put them in the garbage bag.

"Um, Manny," said Eddie as they gathered firewood in the quiet forest, "I'm . . . I'm sorry I said to speak English the other day." He dropped his head. "When the kids at school make fun of me, it makes me ashamed to speak anything other than English."

"Hey, man." Manny stopped tugging at a branch and hopped over the fallen tree. He stood in front of Eddie. "Speaking another language is *awesome*. You shouldn't be ashamed that you know more than those kids at school. They're probably just jealous." His eyes glinted. "Want me to teach you some fun words in Spanish?"

Eddie grinned. "Only if I can teach you some in Mandarin."

When Manny and Eddie returned to the camp with a bag full of dead branches, and Benji hidden behind a pine tree nearby, the rain had finally stopped. Tony and Jake were sitting next to two large pots that had trails of smoke floating above them. Bobby was standing over them, shaking his head.

"I burned dinner," Jake said sadly. "Tony told me that I wasn't using enough water to boil the pasta but I didn't listen to him. Now most of it is stuck to the bottom of the pots." He motioned toward a big red blob on the ground. "And I dropped half the sauce, too."

Manny eyed the spill. "That's okay; it won't go to waste. Ben . . . I mean, been there, done that."

Eddie dumped the sticks out onto the ground. "Now what?" he asked Bobby.

"Now we eat what we can, and then build a fire before it gets too dark," said Bobby. "By the way, you've only earned ten points out of three hundred for your camping skills. Try and make it at least twenty by lighting a decent fire."

After a miserable dinner, the boys tried to start a fire, but even with Bobby's instructions on how to start with small twigs and build up to bigger sticks, and then logs, they couldn't get a flame to catch. As the sun set and the sky turned dark, they gave up and crawled under their tarps and waited for the night to pass.

When Benji was sure that Bobby was asleep, he crept into the camp. He lapped up the spilled sauce and burnt pasta ends hungrily. When he was done, he padded over to Eddie's tarp. He pawed at Eddie's face.

"Hey, Benji," whispered Eddie. He pulled up the tarp and Benji trotted in. He turned a few times and flopped to the ground, snuggling against Eddie. He stayed that way for a while, then got up. Eddie let him out, and Benji went over to Manny's tarp.

That night, Benji used his body heat to keep each of the boys warm. But by dawn, he was back in the woods, ready to follow them when they finally broke camp and headed back to Bunkhouse Ten.

CHAPTER 6

"All right, campers. If we don't do well with today's scavenger hunt, we can say goodbye to any chance of winning the Camp Lakewood trophy," Bobby announced. It was early afternoon on the next day, and the boys had gotten back and unpacked from their survival skills trip.

Bobby held out a sheet of paper. "This is a list of things for you to find. Each item comes with a picture identifying what it is, and each item is worth a certain number of points. Some things are easy, like a maple leaf, and are only worth two points. The harder it is to find something, the more points it's worth."

"What's worth the most points?" asked Tony.

Bobby gave Tony the list. "A Louisiana pine snake. It's worth a thousand points because it's an extremely rare species and no one at Camp Lakewood has ever spotted one before. If you find one, we'll have a chance at winning the week's competition!" He handed Tony an old Polaroid camera. "Whenever you find an item, take a picture of it with this. But leave it where you found it—the scavenger hunt is for finding things, not taking things."

Tony studied the camera. "Wow, this is ancient." He tucked it in his backpack. Then he folded up the list and put it in his pocket.

"Be back by five p.m.," Bobby told them. "And one last thing—you're only allowed to search around the lake. Don't go off into the woods by yourself." He frowned. "Judging from last night, if you get lost, you'll never survive."

As soon as the boys were out of sight of the cabin, a familiar four-legged creature came up to join them.

"Benji!" cried Eddie. He leaned down and ruffled Benji's sides.

"Guys, we can't bring Benji to the lake," said Jake. "If he follows us, the other campers will see him."

"Then we'll go into the woods," Tony declared.

Jake frowned. "Didn't Bobby *just* say 'Don't go into the woods'?"

"We'll be fine," Eddie said. "We've got Benji!" He patted Benji's head and turned away from the lake. "C'mon. I bet we have just a good a chance of finding these scavenger items in the forest as we do by the lake."

As the boys turned and went into the forest, Benji trotted alongside them. After the cold rain of the past night, the warm afternoon sun felt magnificent on his golden fur. Whenever one of the boys stopped to snap a photo of something on the scavenger list, Benji raced around, leaping on sticks and crushing them to a pulp with a giant grin on his face. He loved being with the boys as they tromped through the forest.

He had just finished destroying a particularly big branch, when a flash of movement caught his eye.

"Squirrel!" yelled Eddie. "That's on the list!"

Tony reached into his backpack for the Polaroid camera.

Benji wanted to help out. He pounced . . . and missed. The squirrel jumped between his paws and ran, with Benji hot on its bushy tail. He chased it through the woods, under logs and bushes, until they were out of sight of the boys.

Just when Benji was only a bound away from catching it, the squirrel dashed up a rotting old oak tree. As it scrambled out of Benji's reach, it knocked into a cracked branch. The branch snapped in two, and as it fell, Benji heard a horrible buzzing come toward him. A gray papery nest attached to the branch was exploding with angry hornets.

Before the nest reached the ground, Benji was off and running. He fled straight toward the boys, who were heading in the direction of the maddened insects. He barked and whined, trying to draw them in another direction.

"What's up, Benji?" Eddie knelt down. "What did you see?"

Benji looked in the direction of the fallen nest. A growl rumbled through his throat, low and angry, before turning into a sharp, loud bark.

"Guys, I think he's trying to warn us," said Tony. "Everyone be quiet for a second."

Benji stopped barking as the boys stopped and listened.

"Do you hear that?" said Manny. "It sounds like a million mosquitos."

"Those aren't mosquitos," said Tony. "Those sound like hornets."

"Well, then, let's not go that way," said Jake. "I'm totally allergic to hornets. The last time I was stung by one, I had to get an EpiPen stabbed in my leg."

Benji barked happily as the boys turned in the opposite direction of the nest. He ran ahead of them, making sure to herd them away from the thousands of stinging dangers in the air. As they tromped through the woods, they all found different items on the scavenger hunt list. Eddie found a spiderweb, Manny discovered a butterfly, Tony spotted a bird's nest, and Jake found an animal burrow half-hidden behind a big rock.

As early evening approached, Tony reached into his pocket and pulled out the scavenger hunt list. "We've got almost everything," he announced. "Just the Louisiana pine snake, which we're never gonna see, and a squir . . ."

Benji interrupted Tony with a mighty bark. He galloped ahead of the boys and chased a fluffy-tailed squirrel up onto a high branch of a pine tree. This time, there was no hornet's nest hanging from a branch. As Benji kept the squirrel at bay, Tony held up the Polaroid camera and took a picture. "That about does it," he said.

As Tony was putting the camera in his backpack, Benji let out a hushed growl. He had seen something move under the soft pine needles at the foot of the tree. He sniffed at it, then drew back, whimpering.

A writhing brown-and-yellow snake emerged from the needles. Its head twisted back and forth as it hissed at Benji. Its forked tongue flickered out as it watched him with cold black eyes.

Benji backed away carefully. Behind him, he heard a click.

Tony took three more pictures of the snake, then quickly put the camera away. "C'mon, Benji," he whispered. "Let's get outta here."

* * *

By the time Benji left the campers back at Bunkhouse Ten, they had fed him a hearty dinner of lasagna and sugar cookies from the dining hall. Before he headed back to his little shelter for the night, Tony wrapped his arms around him and gave him a hug. "Thanks for finding that Louisiana pine snake today," he told Benji. "Because we were the only campers to see one, Bunkhouse Ten won the scavenger hunt. We're in second place for the Camp Lakewood competition!"

Benji didn't know what Tony was saying, but he wagged his tail happily. He licked Tony's hands to make sure he hadn't missed any dinner, then trotted home and flopped down to sleep, content with the day's adventure.

CHAPTER 7

Benji woke up the next day panting. The sun was just up, but it was already scorching his fur. It was hot. Too hot to do anything but go for a dip in the lake. He spent the morning swimming next to the doghouse before shaking off his fur and heading to Bunkhouse Ten to see what the boys were doing.

But when he got there, the bunkhouse was empty. Benji sniffed around until he caught the scent of Eddie's chewing gum, then followed it to the edge of the lake, being careful to keep himself hidden.

He found the boys playing with the other campers in the water. Eddie was on water skis, expertly gliding side to side along the wake of the boat that pulled him. Tony and Jake were knee-deep in the lake, tossing a Frisbee to each other. Manny was paddling around the edge of the lake in a kayak.

Benji settled behind a tree to wait for his campers. As morning turned to early afternoon and the boys of Bunkhouse Ten made no move toward coming back to shore, his eyes grew heavier and heavier. He was half asleep when he heard a scream.

Benji was instantly awake. He knew that voice. It was Manny's. He scanned the lake, and saw an upturned kayak in the middle of it. Manny was kicking his legs and sweeping his arms frantically, but despite that, his head kept sinking beneath the water as the kayak floated farther and farther away from him.

In an instant, Benji was out of his hiding place and in the water. He knew that everyone—Bunkhouse Ten, the other campers, and Bobby—could see him, but he didn't care. Manny was in trouble, and no one was close enough to help him. Benji swam as fast as he could, his legs paddling furiously, until he was beside the drowning boy.

He took a deep breath and barked once, loudly. Then he held his breath as Manny grabbed on to him, plunging him under the water. Swimming as hard as he could, Benji let Manny clutch his back. He kept his eyes open, even though they stung, steadily putting one paw in front of the other as he worked his way toward the overturned kayak. When he reached it, he was almost out of air.

Using his last bit of oxygen, Benji powered up

toward the surface of the water. He broke through and gulped in a breath of air as Manny let go of him and grabbed the side of the kayak.

On the water's edge, Benji saw Bobby leap into a canoe and begin paddling out toward him and Manny. Benji knew that if Bobby got to them, he would be in big trouble, but he didn't care. Saving Manny was more important.

Benji looked around and saw the grab handle floating in the water at the front of the boat. In a few short strokes, he was next to it. He opened his mouth and grabbed the handle between his teeth. Then he began to swim toward Bobby.

A few minutes later, Bobby was next to them. Once he had hauled Manny into the canoe, he pulled Benji in as well and grimly tied the kayak to the back of his boat. The boat was dead silent as Bobby rowed them all back to shore.

"You can't get rid of Benji. That's *loco*. You just can't!" Manny shouted.

Benji drew back his ears and whined. He was tied to the foot of Bobby's bed with a long rope, soaking wet and anxious as Manny tried to defend him. After Bobby had taken them back to shore, he had marched them into the bunkhouse and angrily told Manny that he was sending Benji to a pound the next day.

Eddie burst into the bunkhouse. He tried to get to Benji, but Bobby blocked him. "Benji just saved Manny—why is he tied up like that?" he yelled.

Bobby folded his arms. He was about to reply when Jake came running through the door.

"Leave Benji alone!" cried Jake.

Bobby shook his head. "This is the mutt that stole from the dining hall on the very first day of camp with you. I know he helped Manny, but he's a stray. He could have rabies or ticks or who knows what kinds of diseases on him." He looked at Jake. "You, Mr. Worrywart, should be on my side."

"I'm not!" cried Jake. "He's our mascot, and he's fun and great and only a little smelly, and you've got to let him go!"

Bobby stood still for a moment. Then he carefully untied Benji from his bedpost. "You stay here," he told the campers, "and don't move until I'm back." He marched out the door and slammed it shut.

He led Benji away from the bunkhouse and deep into the woods before tying him to a tree. "I'll be back tonight to take you to the pound," he told Benji.

Benji watched sadly as Bobby disappeared back toward Bunkhouse Ten. He tried to gnaw at the rope, but it was too thick to chew through. He sighed and slumped onto the tree roots. He had tried really hard to help the campers, but it looked as if he was going to be taken away from them. He closed his eyes and put his paws over his head.

A moment later, he felt a gentle hand on his back. Benji opened his eyes and saw Tony smiling down at him.

"Hey, boy," Tony said. "I've got to get going, but I know where you are. Me and the other boys will come back for you tonight." He gave Benji a long scratch behind the ears. "I promise."

CHAPTER 8

It was early evening, and the boys of Bunkhouse Ten were gathered around a dining table, plotting Benji's escape while eating their spaghetti and garlic bread.

"I knew Bobby would try and get rid of Benji, so I waited until I saw him leave the bunkhouse," Tony told the others. "Then I followed him and saw where he's keeping him. We've got to get him out of there before Bobby takes him to the pound tonight."

"How do we do that?" asked Jake. "There's no way that Bobby's going to let us get near Benji."

"We'll distract him." Tony quietly explained his plan to the boys as they finished with their dinner.

"It's brilliant," whispered Eddie.

"It's totally gonna work. *Sin duda*," said Manny.

"What's totally gonna work?" called a voice. Bobby was standing over them.

"Our plan to win the Camp Lakewood trophy," said Tony without missing a beat. "All we have to do is win tomorrow's capture the flag contest and we're golden."

Bobby nodded. "Finally! I'm glad you're actually talking about something that matters." He motioned with his hand. "C'mon, let's get back to the bunk-house for downtime."

As the campers followed Bobby to the bunk-house, Jake suddenly began screaming and batting at himself. "There's a hornet inside my shirt!" he cried. He began running back toward the dining hall. "I can't get stung! I'll go into anaphylactic shock!"

Bobby turned and began to pursue Jake. "Calm down!" he shouted. "Don't make it angry!"

Jake yelled even louder and fell to the ground. "It got me! It got me!"

"Jake's got an EpiPen in his storage trunk," Tony told Bobby. "We'll go grab it."

Bobby nodded. "Hurry!" he yelled.

Tony, Eddie, and Manny ran to Bunkhouse Ten.

"You all know what to do," Tony said.

Eddie nodded and ran toward the lake while Manny ran up the cabin steps.

"Stall Bobby for as long as you can," Tony told Manny. He started toward the woods where Benji was tied up.

Manny smiled. "I've got this," he shouted as he disappeared into the cabin.

In the woods, Benji pricked up his ears. He could hear the sound of racing footsteps. His tail began to wag.

A moment later, Tony burst into view. He drew out a Swiss Army knife and swiftly cut the rope away from Benji's neck. "C'mon, boy, let's get you out of here," he said.

Benji jumped to his feet and joyfully licked Tony's face. Then he followed the camper down a path that led to the edge of the lake. He spotted Eddie coming toward them in a canoe.

"Jump in!" called Eddie.

Benji hurtled to the edge of the water and leapt off a rock, landing perfectly inside the canoe.

"Good boy, Benji," said Tony as he got into the front of the canoe. "Now, let's go pick up the others."

As the boys paddled back toward the camp, Benji clawed at the canoe bottom, tried to keep from slipping and sliding. Finally, he found his balance, with his four legs spread out wide as if he was standing in the middle of a patch of ice, and his head poking up over the canoe lip so he could see.

He watched as the canoe headed toward the far end of the camp. There was a figure in the darkening shadows that he could see behind a tree. He squinted and looked closer. It was Manny.

Eddie and Tony steered the boat toward their friend. When they reached him, Manny gingerly stepped into the canoe. He had snuck four life jackets from the boathouse, and was wearing one. He gave Eddie and Tony one each to put on, and then turned toward the shore. "Jake should be coming at any minute," he whispered.

A minute later, Jake appeared, running at a full-on sprint toward them. "He's right behind me!" he shouted as he neared the canoe.

"You were supposed to send Bobby to the infirmary for another EpiPen after I quote unquote 'didn't find yours'!" yelled Manny.

"I did!" Jake yelled back. He was almost at the boat. "But then he saw me get up and started chasing me!"

Benji looked behind Jake. Bobby was hurrying their way—and he looked madder than a whole nest full of hornets.

Benji gave a loud warning bark.

"Hurry!" cried Tony.

Jake leapt onto the boat and pushed off. Tony and Eddie began paddling as fast as they could.

Benji looked behind him. Bobby was at the water's edge already.

"Come back!" he shouted.

"Make us!" yelled Manny. He laughed maniacally

as the campers glided through the water. His face fell, though, when he saw Bobby head toward the boat-house. "Uh, guys, you might want to paddle faster," he said. "Bobby's coming after us."

Benji watched as Bobby hopped in a kayak and began racing toward them. Even with Tony and Eddie paddling furiously, the canoe was heavy and slow. By the time they reached the far end of the lake, Bobby was only a hundred yards behind them.

"Let's go, let's go!" called Tony as he hopped out. He fled into the woods, with Benji and the others close behind.

"You come back with that dog!" yelled Bobby as he slid the kayak onto the shore and jumped out. He crashed through the thick brush after the boys.

Benji and the boys ran deeper and deeper into the woods, pursued by Bobby. Just when they thought they had shaken him and had paused for breath at the top of a steep embankment, they heard the camp counselor's footsteps behind them.

"Gotcha!" cried Bobby. He leapt out from the brush and grabbed at Benji . . . but missed. His arms pinwheeled in the air as he lost his footing and tum-bled down the embankment into a ditch.

"Is he *muerto*?" Manny asked.

The boys were standing over Bobby's motion-less body.

Tony crouched down and put his ear close to Bobby's mouth to check his breathing. Then he gently took Bobby's wrist in his hand. He shook his head. "He's not dead, but he's out cold."

"Something's wrong with his ankle, too." Jake bent over and gingerly touched Bobby's ankle. "It's all swollen."

"We've got to help him," said Tony. He looked at the other boys. "We shouldn't move him until he's awake. He could have a neck injury or something."

"But what if he's out for hours? Does that mean we'll be in the woods alone? With no one to help?" said Jake, his voice rising to a squeak.

Tony nodded. "Look, if we head back for help now we risk getting lost in the dark. We learned a bunch of survival skills the other day. We didn't like learning them, but I think we can use them tonight and leave for help first thing in the morning if he's not better by then." He stood up. "Manny, Eddie, think you can gather some firewood before it gets really dark?"

Manny nodded. "We're on it."

"Good." Tony pointed to Jake. "You and I will go back to the water. There should be a survival kit with first-aid supplies in the kayak. We'll need it to bandage up Bobby. We'll get the life jackets, too, just in case we need them. Let's go before we get lost."

Benji followed Tony and Jake through the brush. When he realized they were heading back toward shore, he led the way. Once they had found the first aid kit and gathered up the life jackets, he guided them back to the ditch.

When they got there, Tony cleaned and bandaged Bobby's head. As he was wrapping up the swollen ankle, Bobby's eyes fluttered open. "What happened?" he groaned.

"You fell down a ditch and hit your head," said Tony.

Bobby sat up. His face paled. He turned his head to one side and threw up. When he was done, he wiped his mouth. "I've got a horrible headache and my ears are ringing," he moaned.

"I think you have a concussion," said Tony. "My brother got one last year playing football and the same things happened to him."

Bobby slowly got to his feet. He had taken only a step or two before he stumbled dizzily. Tony and Jake caught him before he fell. They lowered him to the ground just as Eddie and Manny arrived carrying armfuls of dead branches.

"Bobby's got a concussion and he can't walk," Tony told Eddie and Manny. "We're going to have to stay here tonight." He picked up one of the life jackets. "Let's make something for him to rest on."

Together the boys laid the life jackets on the ground, creating a makeshift mattress. Then they carefully moved Bobby onto it.

"When my brother got a concussion, the doctor told us he could sleep but had to be woken every two hours to make sure he could still talk and his condition didn't get worse. We're going to do the same for you," Tony told Bobby. He turned to Eddie. "Think you can make us a fire for the night?"

"I can try." Eddie rummaged through the pile of firewood he and Manny had collected. He built a small pile of twigs and brush, then used a lighter from the survival kit to ignite it. "C'mon, c'mon," he whispered, coaxing the tiny flame.

"You did it!" cheered Manny as the flame leapt on the pile and burned brighter. He slapped Eddie on the back. "Well done, *amigo*."

Eddie smiled and added a stick to the fire. "Thanks."

That night, the boys took turns making sure the fire was alive, and Bobby was awoken every two hours. And as the hours went by, Benji snuggled up to each one on watch, making him feel safe and loved.

CHAPTER 9

As the early morning sun came through the trees, Benji saw Bobby nodding off. He trotted over to the camp counselor and gently nuzzled his hand. Even though the camp counselor had tied him up, Benji knew he wasn't a bad person.

Bobby smiled weakly. "Hey, pooch." He stroked Benji's head.

Benji leaned over and gave Bobby's face a good slobber.

Bobby laughed and slowly sat up. He gingerly touched his bandaged head. "Ow," he said.

Jake got up from the campfire and went over to Bobby. "You okay?" he asked.

Bobby sat up slowly. "My head still hurts and my ankle is throbbing, but I'll live."

"We should have breakfast pretty soon, and then

we'll need to head back for camp if you're feeling okay," Jake told him and Bobby nodded.

A few minutes later, Tony, Eddie, and Manny appeared out of the woods. Each of them had turned their shirts into pouches that were filled with wild blackberries. They sat down and laid the stained T-shirts down next to Bobby. "Eat up," Tony said.

"Thanks." Bobby grabbed a handful of berries and popped them in his mouth. "These are delicious."

Benji licked his chops and wagged his tail hungrily. He wagged it even harder when he saw Bobby aim a berry in his direction. When the counselor threw it, Benji leapt and caught it expertly in his open mouth. That led all the other boys to toss berries into the air, with Benji racing around as he chomped on his breakfast.

After they had eaten, Tony explained to Bobby how they were going to make a stretcher out of the life jackets and carry him to back to the canoes. Then they would row back to camp and get him to the infirmary.

While they were tying the jackets together, Bobby sat silently, petting Benji, who had laid down next to him to keep him company. Finally, he spoke. "Hey, guys. I just want to say . . . I'm sorry I've been so harsh to you this week. I was so focused on winning the Camp Lakewood competition, I forgot that what mattered more was that you grew in your confidence and abilities. I'm very impressed at how you all stuck together and made it through the night." He looked sheepishly at his ankle. "It just took hitting my head and breaking my ankle to remember that."

The boys were quiet for a minute. Then Tony spoke up. "You know, Bobby, we should also thank you for teaching us the survival skills to make it through the night. If it hadn't been for you, we would have never figured out how to start a fire or use the resources that we got."

Eddie went to Benji and scratched his ears. "We should also be thanking Benji. He's the one who kept us all together. You didn't see it, but before you came into the cabin on the first day, we were ready to tear each other apart. But when Benji came in, we had to work together and keep him hidden. He made us forget our differences and become a team."

"Yeah," Manny said with a laugh. "Me and Eddie were about to kill each other that day. Now we can tell jokes in each other's languages."

Jake nodded. "Benji also taught me how to be brave. I was scared during the night, but Benji made me feel like I was protected."

Bobby gave Benji an extra-long pat. "Well, I guess we owe this guy a lot. Now, let's get back to camp so we can feed him a proper meal."

It took all morning for the boys to build the stretcher for Bobby and carry him to the canoe, and all afternoon before they made it back to camp. By then, it was sunset and everyone only had enough time to shower and eat before bed.

The next day was the last day of camp. After the morning announcements, where Bunkhouse Eight was declared the winner of the Camp Lakewood competition, Benji and the boys returned to their cabin. Since they hadn't been around for the big capture the flag game on the final day of camp, Bunkhouse Ten had come in dead last place.

As they were packing, Bobby came into the cabin. He was hobbling on a pair of crutches. "Hey, everyone, gather round. I have something for you." He held up five glinting homemade medals. "I stayed up all night making these. We may not have won the Camp Lakewood trophy, but you guys will always be my number-one campers."

As Bobby draped the medals over the boys' shoulders, Tony raised his eyebrows. "You made five medals, but there are only four of us."

Bobby smiled and held up the last medal. "This one is for Benji. He deserves it the most, I think, along with this." He reached into his pocket and pulled out a fistful of bacon. "Compliments of the kitchen."

Benji wolfed down his snack and gave a happy bark as Bobby and the campers surrounded him and gave him hugs. As the boys' families arrived to pick them up, he licked each of them on the face. Finally, it was just him and Bobby left in the cabin.

Bobby looked down fondly at Benji. "Hey, boy. Do you want to stay and be Bunkhouse Ten's official mascot?"

Benji paused for a moment. He knew that Bobby was asking him to stay, but the road was calling him again. He woofed and nuzzled his head under Bobby's hand.

Bobby laughed. "All right, then. Good luck out there."

Benji took one last look around. Then he trotted out the door, down the cabin steps, and off onto the road with his tail wagging high.